Three Happy Birthdays

by JUDITH CASELEY

A Mulberry Paperback Book, New York

Watercolor paints and colored pencils
were used for the full-color art.
the text type is ITC Korinna.

Printed in the United States
of America.

First Mulberry Edition, 1993.
10   9   8   7   6   5   4   3   2   1

Library of Congress
Cataloging-in-Publication Data

Caseley, Judith.
Three happy birthdays /
by Judith Caseley
—1st Mulberry ed.
p.   cm.
Summary:
Chronicles the birthday
celebrations of three family
members and what they do with
their favorite birthday gifts.
ISBN 0-688-11699-X
[1. Birthdays—Fiction.
2. Gifts—Fiction.]   I. Title.
[PZ7.C2677Th   1993]
[E]—dc20
92-24583   CIP   AC

For Neil, with love

CONTENTS

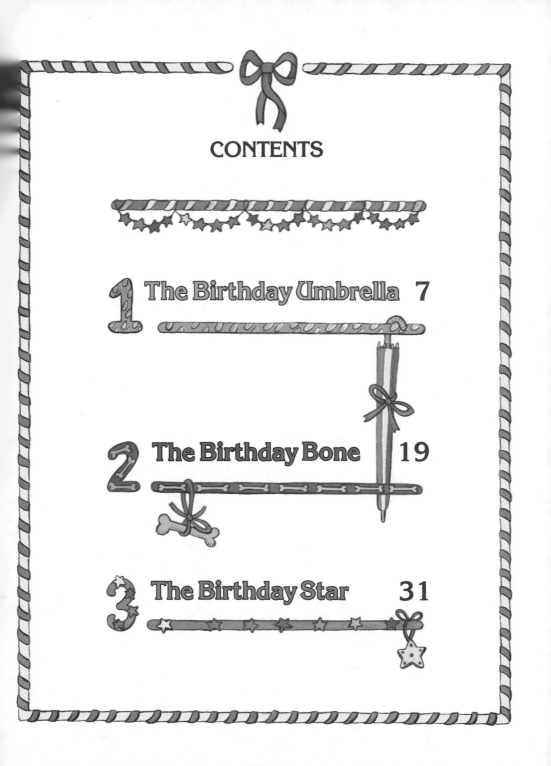

The Birthday Umbrella

It was Benny's birthday.
Mama baked him a cake.
Papa lit the candles.
And Marla helped Benny
blow them out.

They gave him lots of presents.
Benny loved his new umbrella best.

But it didn't rain.

Benny waited and waited.

But he couldn't use his new umbrella.

The ice cream vendor
had an umbrella.

So Benny kept the sun
off his ice cream cone.

The merry-go-round
had an umbrella.

So Benny gave his lion a ride.
Charlie watched.

Benny's friends made believe
they were tightrope walkers.

Benny balanced better
with his umbrella.

And then it started to rain.

So they all went home together.

2

The Birthday Bone

It was Charlie's birthday.

Benny went to the pet shop
to buy him a bone.

Charlie loved his new bone.

He buried it
under the
evergreen tree.

He dug it up again.

He kept it beside him when he ate.

He slept with his bone.

And then he outgrew it.

Benny took the bone.

He washed it.

And he dried it.

He painted it
with shiny paint.

Then he put it on
his bookshelf to remember
when Charlie was little.

3

The Birthday Star

It was Marla's birthday.
Mama baked her a birthday
cake with stars on it.
Marla loved stars.

They made stars
out of paper.

And cookie stars.

And stars out
of snow, too.

Then everyone ate star cookies
and slices of star cake.
And Marla was the birthday star.

Benny gave her a birthday pin.

Marla wore it on her sweater.

She hung it around Charlie's neck.
He didn't like it.

She pinned it
on Benny.
He told her
he didn't want
to be a sheriff.

She wore it
on a ribbon
around her hair.

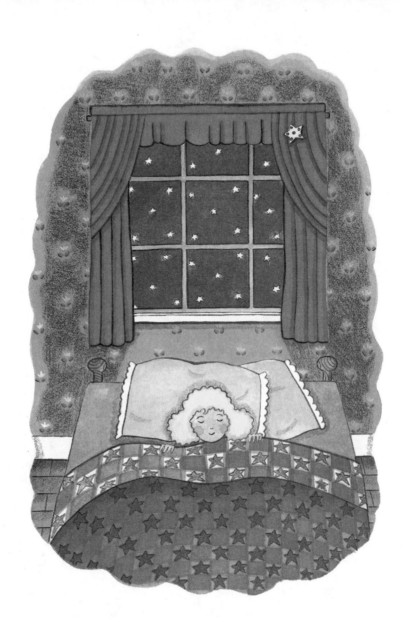

But she liked it best in the sky.
Good night, bright star.